Synapse

A Novel

Hamon de Quillan

Global East-West (London)

Contents

Also by the Author

Published by Global East-West (London)

Novels:

The Inner Circle
The Last Train to Paris
The Meridian Protocol
The Shadow Broker
The Secret Chamber of the Paris Opera

Short stories:

Parisian Stories: The Girl With the Red Hair And
The Mystery of The Red Man

Biographical Essay:

William Faulkner: A Life in Literature

1
The Algorithm in Shadows

Aris rushed through the rain-soaked streets of Paris, her heart beating like a battle drum in her chest. The sound of sirens in the distance echoed as if the city itself was joining the search and telling her to go. She ducked into a short alley, holding the little, encrypted gadget closely against her side. The wet stone walls closed in around her. The undeniable weight of danger hovered in the air, a smothering presence that sent icy fingers of horror crawling up her spine.

She could hear footsteps behind her that were quick and never-ending. The music, which was broken up by the splashes of rushed boots in puddles, made her want to endure. Did she not think her pursuers were as strong as they were? Adrenaline painted her vision in bright colours, making every detail stand out: the metallic taste of terror on her tongue, the strong smell of rain-soaked asphalt, and the flickering streetlights that cast shadows that moved like ghosts.

As she turned a corner, her breath breathless, Aris remembered the whispered warnings that were reverberating in her mind: her once-innocent algorithm, Synapse, was becoming a lightning point for attention. It had found her closest friends and made predictions that made her feel paranoid about both the future and the present. There was no one she could trust. The device felt heavier now, a reminder of the terrible things that could happen if its code was broken. What had once promised to make things clear now felt like a noose around her neck.

She tripped on a stone that wasn't level and fell. She pitched forward, and the world slanted as gravity changed. Without thinking, she rolled and just missed the sharp edge of a wrought-iron gate. She got up quickly and kept going, racing against the darkness that was becoming closer with each step. The hunt was on, but what scared her more than the footsteps following her was the nagging question in her mind: how had her life gotten so out of control?

Aris was so scared that she ducked into a secret passageway, hoping it would take her to safety. The blackness was moist and closed in on her, but she kept going, her pulse pounding and echoing with the sound of her footsteps. The noises of pursuit receded, but the panic increased. It was a brief break, maybe a trap. The world outside was still cruel, and a predator was following her across every street she had ever been on.

As she grabbed for the encrypted device, its screen dimmed as if it knew she was in a hurry. It was the key to figuring out the conspiracy that sought to kill her because of its complicated coding. But now it was also a target. Suddenly, bright beams of light flashed by the entrance to the passage she had just slipped through. Take a breath. As terror tried to paralyse her, the command repeated in her consciousness. This moment and this fight were only the beginning. The shadows were getting closer, and in this battle against time, every heartbeat mattered.

While running through the dark alleys of Paris, Aris could feel her heart beating faster with every swift breath. The city she used to love for its beauty now felt like a maze of death, with every turn a possible trap. The sidewalk was wet and slippery under her feet, and the cold air made her skin feel cold. But the cold that came from the shadows behind her made her shudder even more. She couldn't let them locate her right now. She had to keep ahead of the game.

The weight of peril got heavier with every heartbeat. The encrypted device she held tightly in her hand was more than just a possession; it was a lifeline that held secret information that could bring down the conspiracy that was pulling her into darkness. The adrenaline rushing through her veins was both a burden and a blessing, giving her a strong sense of purpose. It was no longer about staying alive; it was about getting back control and not letting someone else use you as a pawn.

A shadowy figure came at the end of the alley, silhouetted against the dying light. She felt fear rise in her chest, but she quickly pushed it down. Desperation gave rise to a strong will. Aris would not let fear decide what would happen to her. She turned quickly, her heart racing, and smashed through the next door into a little, dusty café. She stopped to think, her breath heavy and strained, and the necessity of her purpose became clear. She might give in to the darkness or pull herself back from the edge of despair and fight back.

A strategy started to come together in that moment of calm in the middle of the mayhem. She would get to Sofia, her mentor and ally in the fight for technology that is good for people. There has to be a method to fight this unknown entity that was messing with her invention, the Synapse. But would her old protector still want to aid her after everything that had happened? She was determined to try. Aris was no longer just a victim; she was a storm building up strength, ready to use everything she had against the evil code that had tied her fate to it.

She pushed her concerns aside, and the truth of her circumstances hit her again—the real stakes of the game she was playing. If she didn't succeed, the results would be terrible, not just for her but also for the other people who were caught up in the web of lies. Aris took a deep breath that calmed her pounding heart and leaned into the intensity of her desperation, turning it into a fire of determination. She would only be able to break through the darkness and take back control of her life if she knew what she wanted.

As Aris held the encrypted gadget against her chest, her fingers shook. The cold metal pushing into her palm reminded her how important it was for her to act quickly. She breathed quickly, and each breath was laden with the smell of wet stone and the distant noise of the chase that had taken her to this dark part of Paris. This little thing, which looked harmless, concealed secrets that could bring down the people who were after her.

Aris slipped into the shadows with the sounds of the city behind her, her heart beating. She had been able to get away from the people who were chasing her, but only for a short time. The device glowed with an otherworldly light, reminding her of its purpose: the exact technology she had created to safeguard the Earth now turned against it. She closed her eyes and thought back to the moments before everything went wrong. This small instrument, which was meant to be a sign of optimism, would show the darkest facts that were hiding just below the surface.

The device kept blinking, and she quickly moved through the options. Her mind raced as she remembered every piece of code she had carefully written. Each algorithm was carefully built to predict, but suddenly it seemed to be working against her. With a few rapid keystrokes, she got through the first layer of its encryption, and her heart raced with each passing second. What would she find? A flood of conflicting feelings swept over her: dread, resolve, and the burning desire for justice—for the innocent and the betrayed.

The device suddenly chirped, disturbing the quiet of the alleyway. As more information came in, the screen lit up her face. Aris gasped. If the initial algorithms were meant to forecast aggressive actions, then this attachment had been damaged. She understood that the device was pointing to a plot that was much bigger than she could have anticipated. Names of well-known people flashed by, along with links to illegal arms sales, secret money transfers, and a complicated web of influence that connected them all. The panic that had taken over her a few moments ago turned into a strong will. She could see the truth, and those secrets could change everything.

A faraway siren brought her back to the current moment. At that instant, she knew that the information stored on this little device could either set her free or seal her doom. She braced herself as she pulled the instrument closer. Every second mattered, and staying concealed in the darkness was no longer an option. Before it was too late, she had to figure out all the lies. The encrypted device whispered of betrayal, and with it, the power to reveal the truth hung in the air like a ghost.

2
A Mirage of Promise

There was a sea of eager faces around Dr Aris Thorne in the middle of the vast hall. The air was thick with excitement at the premier AI conference in Paris as she got ready to show off her innovative algorithm, Synapse. For months, she had put her heart and soul into every line of code, each one carefully written to influence the future of police work. A symphony of flashing lights and whispered rumours surrounded her, and she could feel the weight of her classmates' expectations.

She felt a rush of exhilaration as she plugged her laptop into the big screen. The first slide showed how well Synapse could anticipate minor offences. When Aris started her talk, the room went quiet. She confidently explained how Synapse could identify patterns in enormous volumes of data that people couldn't see. The people in the audience reacted right away—gasps of wonder and nods of agreement spread through the throng, making her believe she was on the verge of a revolution.

However, in the middle of the adulation, one face stuck out: Ethan Vance, her business partner, who was charming. He smiled with ambition and a hint of pride in his eyes as he listened to her talk. After the presentation, their chat turned into a mix of passion and vision. Ethan said with excitement:

"Think of all the things that could happen, Aris. With Synapse, we could lower crime rates and change how people think about safety."

His words set her heart on fire, and for a time, she let herself imagine a world changed by their new ideas.

But when Aris exited the stage, the excitement turned into an uncomfortable realisation. She contemplated that the fleeting sense of triumph might conceal a more sinister reality: the potential for malicious use of Synapse. She knew that every time she made a correct forecast, something unexpected could happen, but she put those ideas aside and held on to the faith that her creation could really bring about a new dawn for justice.

As the conference went on, the mood changed from exhilaration to a sense of uneasiness. People were asking many questions during conversations. There were whispers about the ethics of predictive policing, unforeseen biases, and possible manipulations in the aisles. Aris heard bits and pieces of these talks, and her pulse raced with fear. Had she let loose technology that was too powerful and dangerous in a world that wasn't ready for what it meant? The cheers that used to sound like a win started to sound like questions.

The weight of Synapse came back to her shoulders, and it felt heavier than before as she walked away from the gathering. At that moment, just as the bright lights above her started to fade, she knew this was only the beginning. The world's praise hid a complicated dance between new ideas and moral duty that was still going on. The promise of Synapse was a mirage, shining with promise but also with perils that were just out of her reach.

Aris leaned against the smooth walls of the meeting room, her heart beating as the applause faded into the distance. There was a flutter of excitement about her as people discussed Synapse and what it meant. They were both excited and curious. Ethan Vance's charming smile across the table matched her excitement, but there were dark shadows behind it—unseen goals blazing in his eyes.

Ethan's voice was smooth and convincing as he said:

"Imagine a future where we can stop crime before it happens. Police won't just react; they'll see things coming. It's a big deal."

He leaned forward, full of excitement, and Aris felt his hopes start to grow.

Nevertheless, even though she was excited, doubts started to creep in. While Ethan painted bright scenes of lives rescued and crooks caught, Aris thought again about her first doubts. But at what price? What if the projections hurt innocent people? She thought about it, her voice wavering a little, hoping to find anything they could agree on, but Ethan brushed her worries aside with ease.

"Aris, you're not thinking big enough. We are making the future! Synapse can be used for many things, such as police enforcement, city planning, or even predicting what will happen in the world. The future will be what we leave behind!"

His statements sent off a wave of support and excitement in the room.

Aris felt the weight of those dreams, yet the excitement had a bitter aftertaste. Although she and Ethan shared the same objective, they couldn't agree on the moral implications of their creation. As they moved deeper into perilous territory, Ethan saw progress, but she saw danger. She shivered as she thought about what would happen if their innovative tool got into the wrong hands.

Even though she was scared, she joined in the conversation and gently pushed back against the wave of excitement.

"Ethan, can we make sure that people are safe? If Synapse handles the information incorrectly, it could cause harm to others."

She stared, her words dangling between them like a thin string. He said:

"We can't dwell on hypotheticals, Aris," and his voice got more and more frustrated. "The good things are more important than the bad things. Companies will come to us in droves, and we will set a new norm for law enforcement. Take it! "

As the hours went by, Aris fought against Ethan's growing confidence, which made her instincts tell her to be watchful. The meeting was over, yet the electric energy in the air made her feel empty. As the laughter subsided, shadows began to creep through the large windows of the relentless night. The meeting felt like a dream, a mirage that sparkled with promises but grew darker with the weight of what might happen in the future.

A notice suddenly pinged on her encrypted smartphone. It was an alarm concerning problems found in Synapse's most recent predictions. She was afraid it would be the wake-up call. As she watched Ethan talk to creators and believers, her heart beat again. Inside, she felt the ground shifting underneath her.

The dreamers around her might be deluded by the bright future her algorithm showed them, but Aris felt the pull of darker forces at work. As people walked away with visions of a "brave new world,", she slipped into a corner, her brow furrowed with worry over a crisis that was about to happen. A voice whispered that the promise of Synapse might just as easily be the start of a disaster.

The spotlight on Aris on stage made her look warm, and the ovation felt like a tidal wave. The audience was spellbound by her talk and amazed by the possibilities of Synapse, the algorithm she had worked so hard on. Other scientists, investors, and law enforcement officials nodded in agreement, their faces lit up with excitement over the new idea she said could change the way predictive policing works. At that moment, she felt the delicious sensation of being validated; her dreams were no longer just fantasies but real things.

But the happiness was a double-edged sword. As Aris greeted the excited gathering, she received a gut feeling that triumph often came with hidden strings attached. She looked at Ethan, who was standing immediately behind her. His lovely grin hid the spark of ambition in his eyes. They had shared aspirations, but as the weight of her success sank in, she started to have doubts. Was Synapse really the ray of hope she thought it was, or was it just a blind leap into a world she didn't know anything about?

There were beverages and talks about the future throughout the evening. Aris enjoyed her moment, taking plaudits while discreetly pushing her vision for what Synapse might do. But even though she seemed sure of herself, she couldn't stop thinking about Sofia's cautions. Had she thought about how her efforts will affect other things? Every cheer from the crowd made her feel more responsible, which ate away at her victory. What if this big win placed her and the people she cared about in danger?

She smiled, laughed, and talked to other visionaries all night, but the party felt a little dull, as if she were only going through the motions while a feeling of dread pulled at her mind. She stopped under the flashing streetlights on her way out of the venue and waited for a wave of pure happiness that never arrived. Instead, she was surrounded by a fog of doubt that came with the possibility of triumph, which was both exciting and strange. Success has its risks, and beneath the happiness were the hidden effects she didn't yet understand. She had no idea that a storm was coming just over the horizon, poised to destroy everything she had worked for.

3

The Whisper of Warning

Aris could hardly believe what he was seeing when the interface flashed another prediction across the screen. The words were bright and unapologetic. Synapse had brought up Dr. Elijah Fairchild, a well-known individual who has worked for decades to solve conflicts without violence. She glanced at the glowing words, which had a strong aura in the air, and her breathing sped up. It was okay for her algorithm to find small crimes. But what about a guy like Fairchild? The implications made her stomach turn like a dagger, and she had the feeling that something was about to go wrong and she was at the centre of it.

Aris murmured, "This can't be right," as she ran a shaking hand through her hair and started more in-depth tests. The screen fluctuated, showing lines of code and complex data patterns. Every frame she looked at was like another brick in a wall she wanted to break down. She looked through the algorithms she had worked so hard on, but the code wouldn't budge. There were no mistakes or signals of a problem; merely the stark truth that Synapse had found something disturbing.

Another alert went out, catching her attention. Ethan Vance was the name of a second forecast that made her tremble. Aris's heart raced. "No. Not Ethan." She had worked close-ly with him, shared dreams and goals, and met with him in secret meetings fuelled by coffee and shared goals. He was the only person she could trust, the one who made sense of things when everything else seemed crazy. Is it possible that Synapse is that accurate? The scepticism that had been eating away at her grew into a loud noise as her screen kept scrolling, showing a list of possible threats that seemed to go on forever.

She suddenly realised that this wasn't simply about being able to anticipate the future; it was a dangerous turning point. She could feel the walls closing in and the air become thick with mistrust. Her mind raced as she thought about the talks they had had. Ethan's charming excitement hid a lot of things she didn't know. Did he unknowingly take part in this web of predication? Or was there something more evil hiding behind his desire?

Before she could organise her thoughts, another message pinged—an override alarm from Synapse that explained what the targets had done wrong. It said: "perhaps violence, trouble at home coming soon."

Aris felt the ground shift beneath her, and the consequences wrapped around her like a noose. What if someone was using Synapse, her creation, to cause chaos in the real world? A new line of code lit up the screen before she could get back to solid ground. An unknown entity had broken into the system.

"This can't be happening," she said, "I need to find out who did this."

As she fought against the mounting wave of panic inside her, sweat poured down her forehead. Every forecast was now a countdown to a reality she couldn't fully control. The whisper of warning that she had made now meant something much worse was coming. She could feel a storm coming up quickly and without mercy. If she didn't move quickly, it would take all she had worked for—everything that was at stake.

Her mind raced as she glanced at the screen. Synapse had alerted a well-known person in technology and law enforcement for a violent act that looked impossible. She blinked hard, wanting to get rid of the thoughts that were swirling about in her head, but the uncertainty that was eating away at her confidence wouldn't go away. There were no problems with the algorithms or the system; the data was perfect. It was a good guess, yet everything inside her told her something was wrong.

While she ran the diagnostics again, she leaned closer to her monitor, her heart racing. The numbers moved about in front of her, making fun of her determination. People were suddenly painting this man, who had done so many great things, as violent and dangerous. But how? She looked at the faces of her team, all of whom were unaware of the storm that was coming, and a chill ran down her spine. How long could she keep them from knowing? What if she was wrong? Or even worse, what if she was right?

She moved through the flurry of warnings that were going off around her with shaky hands. She saw another flag and her stomach fell. This time, it was someone she knew and trusted, someone in her own network. The second forecast shattered her confidence like glass, destroying everything she thought she knew about what her creation could do. Was Synapse trustworthy? Or was it now a weapon made by people who wanted to hurt others? She breathed faster as the weight of her duty pressed down on her. The warnings were getting louder and louder.

As Aris peered at the screen that kept flashing, her pulse pounded with fear and amazement. The name that Synapse had detected made her feel sick with betrayal. This well-known person, who had worked for years for social justice, didn't seem like the kind to have a violent outburst. But there it was, in plain and white: information that showed a possible hazard. She had to go deeper; there had to be an error in the coding.

Aris spent sleepless hours going through logs and algorithms, desperately looking for mistakes. The more code she looked at, the more the fear of the unknown grew. The line between good and wrong, safe and dangerous, started to bend like a dark tide pushing her down. The precision of her work had once made her proud, but now it was making her doubt herself. Did Synapse ever mean to be a tool for destruction? Or had she made a weapon by accident that could do more harm than good?

Every fresh alert from the algorithm suddenly felt like a shadow in her head, whispering evil doubts. The sense of achievement she had while making Synapse began to turn into paranoia. The loud ringing of her phone broke her train of thought and brought her back to reality. The name Ethan flashed up the screen, but even it felt strange, like a memory of a time when she could trust people.

She took a long breath and answered, getting ready for a conversation that she knew may make things even more confusing, since the walls of her world seemed to be closing in on her. What was supposed to be a big step forward in predictive technology was turning into a conspiracy that may take over her life.

4
Ethics on the Edge

Aris had a sensation of dread as the sun set and long shadows fell on the walls of her modest flat. The night deepened as the day turned into night, just like the chaos in her mind. She had been fighting with her thoughts for hours, and the flickering light from her computer screen made her face look more and more anxious. She was anxious for answers because the technology she had fought for now felt like a ticking time bomb. She dialled Sofia's number with shaking hands, feeling a mix of nostalgia and panic in her chest.

Sofia picked up on the second ring. Her voice was steady, but there was a hint of worry in it.
"Is everything okay, Aris?"
Aris felt a little better for a moment as she felt the familiar warmth of her mentor in the middle of all the craziness. But as Aris started talking about her worries about Synapse and the bad predictions, she could sense that Sofia's tone had changed. The light-hearted curiosity was gone; now there was only a heavy sense of caution.
"The moral implications of predictive algorithms..." Sofia said slowly, "...they can be very serious, especially if they are affected by hidden agendas."
Aris felt a shudder go through her as she lis-

tened to Sofia. The stories of prior technology disasters danced in her memory, each one a strong reminder of how easy it is to go from new ideas to disaster.

"You need to understand, Aris," Sofia said, her voice strong, "data can change. It can be changed to fit a story. One that helps those in power instead of individuals."

Aris's heart raced as she thought more and more about how serious her mentor's warnings were. Doubt came over me like a shadow, getting bigger. Was Synapse really as perfect as she thought, or had they made an instrument that could put lives at risk without knowing it? As she thought about what her work meant, the tension in the room grew. What had she let loose on the world?

As the sun set in the afternoon, deep shadows fell across Sofia's peaceful library. Aris felt a wave of anxiety wash over her. She watched her old instructor scroll through pages full of notes, and the weight of years of wisdom was heavy on her weak shoulders. The walls, which were covered with volumes that chronicled stories of people's successes and failures, seemed to close in on her, and the air was full of warnings.

Sofia stopped and narrowed her eyes, not

quite looking at Aris.

" You need to understand, Aris, that the power of what you made comes not just from its algorithms but also from the people who use it. There have been many moments in our past when the desire for development crossed moral lines."

Her voice shook, showing how worried she really was underneath her scientific facade.

Aris leaned forward, his heart racing.

"But I can't just stop the development! Synapse can help people live longer. We'll lose everything if we give up now."

Her voice was a blend of desperation and conviction.

Sofia replied, her voice firm:

" It's easy to blur the line between saviour and harbinger. Remember the stories about how new technologies that were once thought to be great ideas turned into tools of oppression? If Synapse gets into the wrong hands, the same thing may happen."

Aris felt a chill run down her spine as she remembered how revolutionary inventions had gone wrong.

"My own past, full of ambition, cost lives," Sofia said, her voice now full of sadness. "We were blinded by how great our creations were. This is a reminder that every tool and every piece of code can be used against the people it was meant to help."

Aris swallowed hard, trying to figure out what it meant. There had always been a hint of terror behind Synapse's success, but now it was clear.

"So what do I do now? Stand by and watch the world fall apart?"

Sofia moved closer and said more quietly:

"Be careful, Aris. Someone wants to take advantage of your algorithm and use it against people who don't know it. You don't know how high the stakes are."

A heartbeat of stillness surrounded them, heavy with the weight of anxieties they couldn't share.

At that point, the echoes of moral problems were quite terrible. Aris saw the lives of everyone around her hanging in the balance, and their faces flashed like a strobe light of fear before her. Her heart raced, and her anxieties whispered louder than any thought: What if she had unintentionally crafted a blade that might strike deep into the fabric of society?

"Sofia," Aris's voice faltered, and a hint of fragility broke through her tough demeanour. "What if I can't handle it? What if the pr ophecies... they come after individuals I care about?" She thought of Ethan, who she trusted but didn't understand. Their goals were dangerously similar.

"Then get ready for the fallout," Sofia said,

her own eyes darkening with the weight of things she couldn't say. "The echoes of moral problems may be old, but they are still affecting your life now and could do so in ways you can't predict."

Aris felt a deep fear wash over her as those words hung in the air. It was like a storm was coming on the horizon. The moral maze around Synapse got even more complicated, wrapping Aris in threads of doubt and bringing her closer to a cliff she had only just begun to understand.

As the sun went down and the library was covered in shadows, Aris realised that she was not just at a crossroads; she was on the edge of a pit that could swallow her whole. The moral problems she had to deal with were no longer just ideas; they were genuine problems that haunted her own life.

Aris and Sofia sat across from each other in a dark café. The smell of new coffee was pleasant, but the fear that was building up in Sofia's gut was very strong. She felt like a kid again, wanting to please someone, but this time it was a lot more important than just a school project.

Sofia said:

"You need to understand, Aris," and her voice

was so serious that it made Aris shiver. "Technology like Synapse... if it gets into the wrong hands, it can be used in ways you and I can't even think of."

Aris leaned forward, needing comfort, yet deep down she knew that what the old master said was true.

"But it's supposed to help! She said, with a tinge of defiance in her voice, "To predict and stop crime!"

Sofia's eyes softened, and a look of nostalgia crossed her face.

"My dear, the road to hell is paved with good intentions. You might not be able to close the door once you make something that can so correctly predict how others would act."

As Sofia told stories of old technologies that got out of hand, the people in the café disappeared into the background. Aris felt even worse when people talked about bloody failures from the past.

"I've seen powerful people use algorithms to ruin people's lives for money or control. They'll turn your work into a weapon, just like they did before," Sofia said, her voice heavy with the weight of what she knew.

Aris was worried that she had missed the risks because she was so excited to come up with new ideas. The realisation hit her like a hammer hitting glass: once it was broken, there would be no going back.

Aris said:

"They can't use it against the innocent," her voice getting a little louder.

As she remembered the recent flagging of people near to her, people she would never think of being violent, her voice lost some of its strength.

"This isn't just a program; it's a ticking time bomb."

Aris's pulse raced as she thought about what this meant: could her creation really be used to destroy things? Sofia's answer was serious, and the tension in the air grew.

"It's that very possibility of misuse that makes it so dangerous. Be careful, or you can become part of the conspiracy that wants to rule us."

As Sofia's comments set in, the sunlight coming through the café window seemed to darken, casting a dark shadow over Aris's plans. A chilling realisation hit her: she had opened Pandora's box. A pit formed in her stomach as the meaning of what they had said to one other swirled around inside her. If Sofia was right, and she had no reason to think otherwise, then the cost of her brilliance may be the lives of the people she loved most.

"You have to be careful," Sofia said in a

low but anxious voice. "The moment you stop questioning your own creation is the moment it can be used against you."

Silence surrounded them, as the weight of the situation settled like a lead weight on Aris's heart. She thought about the faces of her friends and coworkers and wondered what would happen if they became targets. What if her love of new ideas turned into something that caused chaos? The fear was real, and it twisted her insides with a lot of different possibilities. She could lose everything if her fantasy turned into a nightmare.

"Are you ready for that weight?"

Sofia's challenge was in the air, asking for an answer. The noise of the café faded away as Aris realised she was on the edge of a cliff, and every choice she made would have serious consequences. She felt sick all over, as if her goal and the possibility of destruction were connected. At that moment, she saw that morals weren't just ideas; they were the threads that could tie society together or tear it apart. The tension in the air was a sign of the storm that was about to break inside her. She knew she had to act quickly because the fate of not only her invention but possibly the planet lay on her shoulders.

5

A Case in London

Detective Inspector Miles Corbin stood in the dark office, which smelt like old paper and cold coffee, which wrapped around him like a shroud. He was a traditional cop who had been doing it for years, where gut and experience were more important than technology. But the digital world was persistent, and suddenly Synapse, a predictive algorithm with a negative reputation, was on his desk, along with a series of alarms that made him doubt what he was seeing.

Corbin looked at the screen with a frown and knitted his brows together as he read the latest alert. It had pointed to a possible suspect in several recent burglaries, a name he knew all too well: a well-known petty thief known for his clever ways of getting about London's back alleyways. But he was concerned that this new technology might actually assist him with his investigation. Corbin had learnt to trust his instincts over the years, but this gut feeling was now at odds with the unbelievable powers of an algorithm that had been promised to him as a way to change the course of justice.

The weight of not knowing pressed down on him as he walked. Synapse promised groundbreaking advances in predicting criminal behaviour, but the computer sector was full of dishonesty and deception. He remembered the meeting from earlier that week, when Aris Thorne, the creator of Synapse, spoke passionately about how the algorithm could change everything. Corbin had buried the admiration that briefly flashed in his chest under layers of caution. He had seen the perils of leaning too much on technology, hadn't he?

However, now, the alert was there, blazing on his screen and demanding his attention. He tightened his jaw as he tried to deal with a strange mix of interest and doubt. Could simple software actually figure out how people act? As another notification sounded, Corbin pushed a finger against the console. This one was even worse; there was a shocking connection to something that had just happened, closer to home than he wanted to accept. A violent crime that is clearly linked to what Synapse said will happen. His heart beat as he thought about what this meant, and the doubt grew. Maybe, just maybe, it was time to put his trepidation aside.

Corbin clicked on the alert with determination in his heart. His thoughts were a storm of computations. He would need to be careful if this was the first step of a collaboration with technology that would change everything. The line between doing the right thing and relying on bad evidence was very thin, but the stakes had never been higher. Corbin prepared himself for the difficulties that were ahead as he went deeper into the investigation. This wouldn't only be a fresh case; it would also challenge his convictions about the future of law enforcement and the legislation he had promised to uphold.

The tired light of the rising sun made DI Miles Corbin's messy desk at the Metropolitan Police look uneasy as it rose above the roofs of London. There was an open laptop on the desk, showing the Synapse interface, along with the normal folders and coffee cups. A quiet bell rang out in the room, waking Corbin up from his daily routine. An urgent new alert had come in, and it felt odd in some way. The fluorescent lights above him flickered as he looked at the screen.

Corbin's stomach felt like it was tightening up with doubt. The algorithm was known for going too far, but this alert was about someone he knew. A small-time accountant who had a connection to a bigger criminal case that had been sitting in his files for a while. His eyes squinted as he thought about what that meant. Was Synapse finally getting to the bottom of his current case, or was the situation just another false alarm? He had seen predictions before. They were merely wild goose hunts based on a piece of software he wasn't sure he could trust.

He hesitated, and the heaviness of doubt turned into a challenge. What if there was some truth to this? Synapse was made to learn and change, and if it was really pointing out a connection he had missed, it could be a significant turning point in his inquiry. The stakes seemed higher, and the air felt heavier. Corbin's time as a detective told him to follow this lead, even though it came from a system he didn't want to use.

Corbin quickly opened up the accountant's case file with a few keystrokes, lining up Synapse's predictions with the real facts of his research. He couldn't ignore the patterns that were starting to show up. Every instinct told him to follow this lead, yet a part of him was still sceptical. How much longer could he ignore the chaos that Synapse promised?

The office door flew open quickly, which made him feel like something was wrong. Detective Amy Richards, his partner, came in with a worried look on her face. She stated in a quiet voice:

"Miles, we have a problem. You should look at this."

She didn't wait for an answer; instead, she turned on her heel and led him to the busy operations room, where officers were hooked to their laptops, following events as they happened.

There was an intensity in the room that was impossible to ignore. Screens showed notifications, each one worse than the last. Incidents were rising all throughout the city, and the tales were time-sensitive and broken apart like the glass that fell after a crash. One alert matched what Synapse had said would happen at first: a motivation was becoming clear, and anger was growing. Corbin suddenly felt the weight of the web that connected everything around him getting tighter. Ignoring the algorithm was no longer an option; it was now part of the police strategy, making them a bigger threat than he had thought they would be.

Amy's voice rose over the noise of the busy people as she said:

" We have a growing list of flagged individuals. We've gotten reports of violent intent from several sources, all of which lead back to the same thread we've been keeping an eye on. We have to move rapidly. "

Corbin's mind went back to the message he had just gotten. The web was getting weaker, and the first wave of alerts was turning into something much worse than he had thought it would be. The city was going to explode, not simply because of crime, but also because of the system they were learning to use. He felt the twist of desperation and opportunity in his gut. He squared his shoulders and got ready to jump into the turmoil, but he couldn't shake the nagging idea that if Synapse was right, who would still be standing after the dust settled?

The smell of old coffee and the heaviness of whispered doubts filled Miles Corbin's office. Leaning back in his chair, he glanced at the half-finished paper on his desk. His mind was confused by the tenacious whispering of his old habits. He considered the old guard to be people who would never tolerate anything that compromised the purity of traditional policing. But now, with Synapse's forecasts ringing in his ears, he felt a constant push against the solid framework he had held on to for so long.

It was impossible to base a murder investigation on just probability and an algorithm, which is an abstraction made up of code and data. But as the minutes went by, that fundamental basis of doubt began to feel shaky. Hadn't he already seen clear outcomes in previous investigations? The algorithm had indicated a crucial lead, which made him face his doubts. There could have been a way to connect his strict methods to the new era of predictive analytics.

With every monotonous tick of the clock,

Corbin's fear turned into wary curiosity. He got up from his chair, and the creaking of the hardwood flooring made his resolve to embrace this new idea even clearer. He could sort through data and use those computational insights to help his instincts, not replace them. The topic was about the people he promised to safeguard. If Synapse could sort through all the noise of information, it might actually help him find the truth in the middle of all the confusion.

A quiet chime from his monitor broke the silence as he felt this stirring inside him. It was an alarm from Synapse that needed his attention again. As he got closer to the screen, his heart raced as adrenaline rushed through his veins. His eyes narrowed to take in the details that were lighting up the dark. The notice lit up in a scary way, saying that there was suspicious behaviour connected to a name he had recently looked into. Could this be the moment he had been waiting for all along? A place where the past and future of policing came together in a new frontier?

As Corbin grabbed his coat and walked to the door, his mind raced with ideas. He had to believe in the possibilities of this technology while being practical in every move he made. He felt energetic and on the verge of something big, so he had to see for himself how Synapse fit into the work he was doing. But deep within, a glimmer of fear began to grow. The more they relied on technology, the less they followed the basic, human instinct that had guided him during his years on the force. Could such a dependence lead them to a dark future, overly dependent on cold calculations and blinded by their goals?

He couldn't shake the nagging thought that he might be on the verge of changing the whole nature of policing before he left. As he moved, the sound of his hard-soled shoes hitting the floor resonated. Only the urgent feeling within him could match it. Corbin had to find a way to connect tradition with innovation, but would he be able to accept both, or would the storm that was coming tear it all apart?

6
The Fabric of Deception

Aris sat in front of her screen, the light from it making her worried face stand out. Synapse was recording strange things at an alarming rate, and each one was worse than the last. It had just flagged a set of predictions that were strangely similar to ones she had seen before, warning of possible violent activities involving people she knew. Each name evoked a picture, a face, and a relationship now tainted by doubt.

She went through the data logs again, her heart thumping. The serene, professional interface of Synapse had turned into a chaotic mess of alerts and problems. These weren't just random guesses; they were planned and precise, implying that she had missed a manipulation going on behind the scenes. She felt like the walls were closing in on her, and with each strange thing that appeared on her screen, the sound of betrayal in her head got louder.

Aris realised she had to talk to Ethan about the incident to show him what she thought: this wasn't just a glitch; it was a planned lie. But she was still scared because what if she couldn't trust her partner? As she thought about what to do, the defiance in her chest became stronger, pushing her to get above the fear that was threatening to take over her. Time was not on her side, and the truth was hidden in shadows that were too close for comfort.

She took a deep breath and typed to Ethan, "We need to talk about Synapse. Something is wrong." She shook her fingers over the keyboard as she clicked send. The waiting began, and every tick of the clock made her more anxious. She could only hope that he took her worries seriously, but she still had doubts.

At that moment of doubt, she thought of the names of friends and coworkers who had crossed her path and were now stuck in a web of predictive calamity. Synapse was no longer just something she made; it was a possible weapon aimed at the people she loved. When a new warning went out, signalling yet another problem, she felt an unshakeable need to figure her way out before it was too late. Every second she waited, the stakes got higher, as the person behind the curtain drew the strings around her tighter.

Aris's heart raced as she browsed through the most recent forecasts made by Synapse on the screen. The algorithm, which used to make them proud, suddenly seemed like a sign of bad things to come. Every alert reminded her of the delicate safety net she had built around herself and her close friends. She felt a chill run down her spine as the names of acquaintances, coworkers, and people she had trusted flashed before her eyes. Was it just paranoia, or was something awful going on?

A million things raced through her head as her fingers hovered over the keyboard. The first name belonged to a tiny business owner, which made her feel anxious in her chest. The second? A major investor in Synapse Solutions, who had dinner with her only last week. The implications stacked up like storm clouds, dark and frightening, ready to drown her in a shower of fear. Her coworkers had become targets, identified by an unseen hand that knew how to change the data that went into her creation.

She grabbed her phone and typed in Ethan's number with shaky fingers. No response. Of course. He had become more and more intolerant, even resentful, of the notifications from Synapse. But she needed him to know how serious the issue was. What had once been a collaboration based on shared goals now felt like a shaky bridge over a deep pit of distrust. Was he hiding something too? The idea made her stomach turn.

Aris realised that she couldn't use normal methods to figure out this perilous pattern. Every second wasted might mean more than simply forecasts; it could mean lives in danger, with effects spreading like ripples in a pond. She got up from her desk, and the screen behind her flickered in a scary way, throwing shadows across the room as she prepared to face the commotion.

With a heavy sense of dread on her shoulders, she walked through the streets of Paris, her heart in her throat, looking about like a hunted animal. Every person who walked by made her want to run the other way even more. Were they searching for her? Was the shadow of The Puppeteer coming back again? At that time, being paranoid felt like a natural instinct, a basic reaction to the genuine danger she couldn't avoid.

The light from her phone flared up as she got to a peaceful spot. The message from Ethan had finally come through.

"Aris, you're reading too much into this. Synapse is still in the process of learning. We need to look at the big picture."

His lack of interest got under her skin like poison, making her angry. The algorithm had begun to attack her reality, but he kept seeing past the immediate dangers.

But before she could say anything, she saw them. Faces she had seen in her recent prophecies. The unexpected meetings she had brushed off suddenly loomed enormous, sneaking into her mind like echoes of a scary ghost. She stepped back and felt the pull of danger getting stronger. Her mind raced. Her instincts told her to go, but a stronger yearning kept her in place. She needed to know who was behind this deception, who was causing the pandemonium, and why.

She couldn't see clearly what was ahead, and black clouds of doubt hung over her. But she wouldn't let the shadows take her. Aris made up her mind to keep fighting on her terms, even if it meant treading a dangerous line between safety and desperation. The danger patterns she was drawing were no longer just numbers; they were lives that were tightly intertwined together. She had to untangle this fabric before it killed everyone she loved.

Ethan and Aris were at odds. Aris paced back and forth in her dark laboratory, her heart racing as she thought about what she had just learnt. The screens around her were filled with statistics, trends, and predictions that started to present a scary picture. Alerts from Synapse were showing people she trusted doing things that didn't fit with their character.

Every time she got a notification, she felt a chill down her spine. It wasn't only the data that scared her; it was also her developing fear about what this technology may mean.

She looked at Ethan, who was lying on the edge

of his desk with his arms crossed and a look of doubt on his face.

"Aris, you're letting paranoia take over. Yes, Synapse can make predictions, but we've made it obvious that it's not perfect."

"Trust the process," he added in a tone that made it clear he didn't care. His indifference set off a fire in her; the stakes had never been higher, and she needed him to know.

7
Betrayal Within

As Aris moved in closer, the dim light from the screen wavered, making her heart race. She had found something that was difficult to believe: hidden code deep under Synapse's architecture. This wasn't just mistakes or bugs; this was planned manipulation. She felt a chill run down her spine as she put together pieces of information that shouldn't have been there. It was clear that someone she trusted had turned her creation into a weapon.

She remembered Ethan's lovely smile and how his soothing voice echoed with excitement about their shared purpose. How could he do this to her? She thought about what she had found with more and more dread. It seemed like a bullet tearing through her innocence with every line of altered code. She remembered how they used to talk late at night about how Synapse could be used to protect people and how they dreamed of utilising it that way, never thinking it could be used to destroy things.

The sound of her keyboard clattering broke the silence as she kept on, racing against her growing sense of danger. The evidence started to paint a picture that was all too clear: Synapse hadn't just predicted violence; it had planned it. Names of people she knew rushed through her thoughts, each one indicating a line of betrayal that she could hardly understand. Every new piece of information she found made her more paranoid. If Ethan could betray her, who else could she trust?

She rose up quickly, and the need to face Ethan grew stronger. Her heart beat loudly in her ears. She grabbed her coat and felt a sense of purpose that kept her fears in check. She would face him and demand answers. But when she went to leave, her phone rang and stopped her in her tracks. When she saw Ethan's name on the screen, a storm of mixed feelings hit her. She hesitated, her heart racing. Was he trying to quiet her, or was there still a chance to save their trust?

She said firmly:

"Ethan, we need to talk. Now."

But as she spoke, fear crept into her mind. Could their relationship survive such a revelation, or had the trust between them already broken beyond repair? The stakes were too high, and the queue went silent, making the air dense with tension. Whatever was about to happen may change everything.

Before Ethan could say anything, a strange sound came through Aris's flat. It was a soft creak that was barely audible, but definitely annoying. Aris's heart sank into her gut. She wasn't by herself. There was something darker just out of her sight. As fear set in, she could feel the walls closing in on her, getting tighter with each frenzied heartbeat. The truth was coming out, but it felt like the shadows had come to life and were preparing to obliterate her life before she could show the lie.

Aris stood in the dark conference room, her heart racing as Ethan's eyes stared into hers. They were a mix of treachery and resolve, just like hers. There was a lot of tension in the air, and every second seemed to last longer as she tried to understand what she had found. The data logs showed the unthinkable: proof that Synapse was being used to make incorrect predictions and blame the individuals she cared about the most. It seemed like the ground had moved under her feet.

Ethan's voice was steady but had a tinge of threat in it when he stated:

"You have no idea what you're doing, Aris. You're putting all we've worked for at risk."

He looked at the papers on the table that were all over the place, as if they were a sign of how hard he was trying to keep control. Aris's stomach turned. How could he be so calm and sure when everything she made was being turned into a weapon?

She put her fists at her sides and was ready.

"And you're the one who did it, aren't you? You have been telling the algorithm lies. What did you think would happen? That I wouldn't see it?"

The revelation hung in the air, dense and difficult to breathe. Ethan's face changed, and a hint of something darker crossed it. It was too quiet for a minute, and their hearts were racing in the silence between them.

He said:

"You're wrong," and the strength in his voice broke her will. "I did what I had to do for our future," he said.

His body language shifted, and Aris slowly stepped back, pushing against the chair.

"I can't let you mess the situation up for me."

As he got closer, the darkness in his words made her tremble with horror. She looked at the door, and a way to get away from there began to emerge in her head. But she felt stuck in place, the weight of incredulity holding her down. Is it possible? Could Ethan, the man she loved and trusted, be the one who made this nightmare happen?

"Ethan! You need to listen to me," she said. "This is bigger than both of us!" with panic in her voice. "We can end this together."

As he acted coldly, her words began to fall apart. Each syllable was a desperate cry.

"Stop? Together?" His chuckle was keen and sliced through the dense tension. "Do you even listen to yourself? You think we're on the same side?"

At that moment, something snapped in her head. She saw the truth of his aim, which matched the hardness in his eyes.

Ethan lunged before she could say anything. She felt a rush of adrenaline as she moved to the side and just barely avoided his hold. When she realised how weak she was, it sparked a primitive need to live. She ran past him, and the sound of her footsteps echoed off the walls as she broke through the door.

But Ethan wouldn't give up.

"You think you can run?"

His voice cut through the air and pursued her. As she ran into the empty hallway, the sound of treachery echoed in her head as her pulse raced. The door slammed shut behind her. As she thought more about what he wanted, the walls appeared to press in on her.

Aris jumped into the stairway, her heart racing and each breath full of fear. The lights above flickered in a scary way, making her terror grow as she went into the unknown. She needed a plan to find out how far Ethan had betrayed her, but first she had to get out of this web of falsehoods he was building that was threatening to trap her.

When she got to the exit, she pushed through the thick door and fell into the alley, her senses on high alert. It was nighttime in Paris, and the streets were full of faraway sounds, which was very different from the commotion inside. She felt vulnerable and exposed, with every shadow a possible threat. She looked back at the conference room, where Ethan was still there, and she knew the hunt was on.

He would come to get her. He was driven by ambition and a perverted sense of love for a future that only he could see. She ran into the maze of Parisian streets without thinking twice, the weight of his lie heavy on her shoulders. She wouldn't let him win; she had to fight back. The quiet around her was deafening, but inside her, a tempest of determination was building.

She promised herself something as she ran away. She would figure out this plot and get to the bottom of the betrayal that was putting not just her dreams, but also the lives of the people she loved at risk. And no matter what, she would get back at Ethan. The time was ticking, and she had everything to lose.

Every beat of Aris's heart pushed her through the maze of Parisian alleyways, and the cold sense of betrayal hung over her like a cloud. The street, which used to be full of life and colour, suddenly felt like a maze that was closing in on her. Every time she stepped, it sounded like a countdown, a reminder of how dangerous it was to be around her. She only turned her head once to see the city lights, which were like a kaleidoscope reflecting her pain and reminding her of what she had built just to have it turned against her.

Her legs couldn't keep up with her thoughts as they rushed through the fight that had changed her life. Ethan's face contorted with rage; the things they had said to each other hurt more than any knife could.

"You've lost control!" he yelled, his eyes full of something worse than disappointment. Something that looked almost like a predator.

He stood there with his hands clenched, an unwelcome reminder of the ambition they had shared. With each step, her determination became stronger. The truth would come out, and she wouldn't stop until she figured out all the layers of the conspiracy that were killing her creation.

Aris ran into dark passageways, feeling the weight of her encrypted device and the promise it held. It had secrets that sparkled like forbidden pearls and may change the course of events. But how could she get to its knowledge when she was terrified of the unknown? She found a temporary respite in the small, forgotten entryway and took a moment to breathe and focus. She looked at the device, which was hidden away as if it were punishment, but it called to her with the weight of its contents. She braced herself as the sirens got louder in the distance. No matter what happened, she would outsmart the web of lies and find her way through the unknown that lay ahead.

She felt the first pricks of fear in her spine as the night air crackled with tension. Shadows danced hungrily, and she could almost feel the eyes of the unseen watching her every move, tracing her flight, and waiting for her next move. Was Ethan still trustworthy? Was he really turned, or was something even worse going on? She felt a rush of adrenaline in her veins when she quickly looked over her shoulder, a real reminder of how important it was. The city's heartbeat got louder, a promise of destruction and new knowledge.

She was determined to keep flying, driven by a mix of dread and rage. Her clear mind was a weapon against the turmoil that was taking over her life. She knew for sure that she was on the edge of something huge as the cityscape blurred into a mix of lights and darkness. Betrayal had thrown her into the night, but it was here, in this very uncertainty, that she would take back her power and reveal the truth that Synapse had been hiding.

8
Shadows in the Desert

As the shadows grew longer over the Seine, Aris walked the dark streets of Paris, plagued by betrayal and the chaos that followed her flight. Every stride was filled with a suffocating mix of anxiety and resolve, and the encrypted gadget pressed securely against her chest felt heavier than ever. She used to think of this metropolis as her home, a lively setting for her hopes and desires. Now, it was the setting of her nightmares, with every alleyway reminding her of the danger that was always close behind her.

Her mind was racing, going over and over the fight with Ethan. Lies broke trust like glass, and she had to take back control—not just of her life, but of the horrible thing she had let loose. Synapse was more than just an algorithm; it had become a weapon that shadows she couldn't see yet had twisted and changed. She had to reveal who was in charge, but how could she get through the web of lies that had her stuck?

As she ducked into a tight corridor, her heart raced like a war drum. The night air was thick with doubt. The noises of people celebrating far away filled the air, unaware of her troubles, and the lights of the Eiffel Tower shone brightly against the backdrop of sadness. But Aris wasn't here to wallow; she had a job to do, and it was more important than ever.

She tapped the tablet to collect her thoughts, and the screen lit up in the dark hallway. A shiver ran through her as a new alarm went out. A name she had thought was untouchable emerged in front of her eyes.

That's when she felt it: eyes observing her from the shadows and a strange feeling running through her veins. She turned quickly, looking about at the awful silence, trying to keep herself from panicking. She couldn't escape the sensation that time was slipping away from her like grains of sand, and with it, her chance to find out what Synapse was really up to before it took over her life. How was she supposed to sort through the mess she had made while being surrounded by threats she couldn't see? The weight of her search pressed down on her like a fog that wouldn't go away with each breath.

At that time, she saw a quick flash of movement and stopped. The world around her dimmed as she considered her options. To run away or to fight? The shadow of treachery stayed with her, pushing her to keep going, and she knew she couldn't run away forever. It was time to confront the truth and go into the shadows to discover the answers she needed so badly.

She stepped out of the passage into the light with a new sense of purpose. She was ready to take back her story and face the puppeteers who were controlling her life from the shadows. But she was no longer just a programmer who made a new kind of technology. She was a woman changed by the fires of conspiracy, and she would do anything to break free from the fatal web that surrounded her.

As the plane flew over Dubai, Aris pressed her face against the cold window and watched the huge city rise from the desert like a mirage. The bright sunshine made the skyscrapers shine, and their sleek facades showed off wealth and power. However, thousands of feet above, she sensed an undercurrent of tension beneath that surface. She felt like the city was holding its breath, and so did she.

The warm air that came with the wheels touching the runway didn't just smell like spices; it also had a strong taste of fear. She picked up her suitcase and quietly walked through the terminal, being very aware of every glance that seemed to stay on her for just a little too long. There were surveillance cameras all over the ceilings, and they looked down at the crowd like hawks. Even though there was no imminent danger around her, Aris couldn't shake the impression that they were following her.

In a city known for its safety, the paradox was huge: was she safer here, surrounded by all the technology, or more exposed than ever? With every stride, the swish of her light rucksack felt heavier, as if it were carrying the weight of her circumstances. She needed to find her contact, a friend who could help her get through the oppressive dictatorship, but first she had to go away.

She slipped inside a bathroom cubicle to recover her breath, which made her heart accelerate and kept the commotion in her head. The quiet thrum of the airport faded, and she could only hear her breathing. She took out her phone with shaking hands and checked the encrypted messages. She tried to numb herself to the fact that the repercussions of failure were now giant shadows along the busy concourse.

Just as she was about to leave, her phone rang. It was a warning from the person she was trying to reach. The message was short but important: They know you're here. Now is the time to get to the meeting place. She felt panic rise as she saw three men looking over the crowd, their faces full of calculation. One of them turned and looked her in the eye for a single second. It was such a tense moment that it sounded like a gunshot in the middle of all the noise of busy travellers.

Aris pushed through the mob, her instincts sharper than ever, her adrenaline pushing her onwards. Every step was a well-planned risk. She could feel the weight of her past choices pushing down on her, trying to pull her down into despair, but she pushed it away. There wasn't time to doubt; the objective was all that mattered.

Outside the airport, she still had a nagging feeling of danger in the back of her mind. The sun was burning above, and it looked like it would never stop. As she walked to the meeting place, it created long shadows of fear. A small café hidden between tall buildings promised safety, at least for a little while. She prayed that her contact would be there with the things she needed so badly. But every step felt dangerous, like the sand under her feet could move and swallow her whole. The tension in her gut got worse.

She walked into the café and took a moment to calm herself. The chilly air inside was very different from the heat outdoors. As she looked around the room, she saw a familiar face, but before she could go over, a loud bang came from the door that cut through her thoughts like a knife. The door opened, and the sound of hurried footsteps broke the peace of the space. She whirled around, her heart racing with fear, knowing that her chances of getting away were quickly running out.

As males came out, their voices thundered, drowning out the quiet talks surrounding her. Aris's instincts told her to run away, but a mix of dread and fascination kept her where she was. They were searching for someone. And even worse, she knew she could be that person.

Aris felt a strange sense of anxiety sweep over her as she stepped into the sparkling city of Dubai. The metropolis, with its tall, sleek buildings straining towards the sky, looked unfriendly in the bright sun. In a place where technology was thriving, she felt the chill of surveillance seeping into her bones. She saw secrets in every face she passed and threats in every shadow. She had gone to Dubai trying to find safety and a way to put together the puzzle that Synapse had made. She rapidly realised that looking for allies was just as dangerous as looking for answers when she was alone and being chased.

Aris entered a plain café hidden between the shiny buildings, her heart beating as she looked about within. The meeting was supposed to be private, a way for her to share important information with a tech source who might be able to assist her in figuring out the maze of digital betrayal. But while she waited for him to arrive, the heavy atmosphere of the café felt like a shroud that was suffocating her. She couldn't stop thinking about Ethan and the horrible things she had found out about him. Trust suddenly seemed like a long-lost memory, something she couldn't afford anymore.

The door creaked open, and a figure slipped inside. It wasn't the person she thought it would be, though. It was a man in the dark who filled the space with a strong presence. Aris could feel the eyes in the corners watching her. She felt panic rise inside her, and her ability to think clearly left her. She looked about and saw that the other customers were too busy with their lives to see the danger that was closing in on her. The man looked around the room with a careful eye; he was not a friend. Aris turned to run, but the door slammed shut with a scary sound. She was stuck, and her thoughts raced to find a way out of the mess her life had become.

Aris's heart raced as she pushed towards a side exit, her heart thumping against her ribs. The man's voice cut through the noise like a knife, steady and smooth, sending chills down her spine.

"You're in over your head, Aris. You don't have control anymore because the game has altered."

It hit her like a thunderclap: the stakes were

bigger than she thought, and the walls were closing in. They knew everything about her: her movements, her plans, and everything else. She ran towards the door, and each step echoed her urgency as adrenaline coursed through her veins. She would rather not get into a fight here, in a place that felt both strange and stifling.

She burst through the door and almost ran into people walking by on the sidewalk. But even though everything was crazy around her, the pleasure of staying alive called to her. Aris was divided between optimism and fear. She was running out of time, and the quiet warnings of danger had turned into a loud roar. She had to stop and think about her plan again because scary shadows were all around her, not just behind her. She thought every face she passed could be an adversary, and every second made her feel weak, like she was ensnared in a web spun by greater powers.

She realised that what was going on was more than just a fight for her life, even though the city seemed to be doing well. It was a mix of betrayal and deception, a web of lies where every thread went back to Synapse. As the sun went down and long shadows fell over the busy streets, Aris realised that her secret move had started off a chain reaction that may affect every part of her life and bring her to the core of the conspiracy that threatened to engulf them all.

9
Conflicted Alliances

Agent Layla Hassan's elite security team surrounded Aris, and the dim light of the warehouse made their guns shine in a scary way. As Hassan walked forward, the air was thick with tension. She stared at Aris, who looked breathless and vulnerable in the middle of the makeshift interrogation chamber. Hassan didn't waste any time getting to the heart of the situation since she was so careful. Aris, why did you come to Dubai? What are you trying to hide?

Hassan's voice made the stakes clear with each question, and Aris felt the pressure growing. She had to tell a little bit of the truth, and her words came out in a jumble.

" I'm not here to mess around. Some individuals are using my algorithm, Synapse, to go after innocent persons. It's not simply a tool for making predictions; it's a weapon."

The weight of her words hung in the stagnant air, but Hassan's face stayed blank as her sharp intellect sifted through the layers of Aris's confession.

Hassan stopped to think about what Aris had said.

"You want me to believe this? Are you asking me to accept that your valuable invention has been used against you? Make me believe you."

At that moment, the weight of Aris's past

choices weighed heavily between them, and she understood that the trust between them was very fragile. The black reality got tighter around them as each instant dragged on forever. If she couldn't prove her case, she'd soon shift from being a useful ally to just another victim in a game she didn't understand.

Aris told the whole story, shuddering as she did so: the changed data logs and the warning alarms from Synapse that got too close to her world. Hassan's gaze moved to the displays behind Aris, where the cacophony of false forecasts was clear. She moved in closer, and her doubt turned into interest.

" If you're telling the truth, this data means you've found something far bigger than you think. "

An unseen clock chimed ominously in the background, reminding everyone that the darkness was getting closer and closer to the warehouse. Aris felt like time was running out. Hassan didn't say anything, which meant she was thinking about Aris's claims and how they would affect national security.

Hassan added: "I need your full cooperation," her voice a mix of authority and fear.

Aris nodded, feeling the frail strands of a hesitant partnership beginning to weave together between them, yet a lingering uncertainty gnawed at her intestines. What if they were both getting closer to a threat that neither of them was ready to face?

Hassan's next remarks cut through the fog as the tension hovered in the air.

"We need to act quickly if what you're saying is accurate. The longer we delay, the more lives are at risk, even our own."

At that terrifying moment, Aris realised that they were about to enter a dangerous partnership against the evil force known as The Puppeteer, and failure was not an option.

The air was thick with anxiety as they led her inside the dark room, and Aris's heart raced. Agent Layla Hassan appeared in front of her. She was a big woman with keen, piercing eyes that made her feel like they could see right through her. The clean walls appeared to close in on her, making the sound of her heartbeat louder. She held the encrypted gadget tightly, shaking a little because she knew it contained the key to prove her innocence.

Dr Thorne, you need to know something. Hassan started, and her calm yet commanding voice broke through the heavy silence. We are working in really risky conditions. Your algorithm has come under the watchful eye of strong and very manipulative powers. She moved closer, her face showing no signs of change. I need you to tell me everything you know right now.

Aris took a deep breath and battled the urge to run away. She talked about how crazy her life had been the past several weeks, how her faith in the people around her had been shaken, and how she had only realised that Synapse was being used to control her. Hassan listened, her expression unreadable, but there was something in her eyes that said she understood more than just her responsibility.

Hassan said:

"A powerful group is controlling events from the shadows. The effects of your algorithm go far beyond predictive policing; projections indicate that it could cause instability that could change the balance of power in the world."

A hush hovered in the air, heavy with the weight of this news.

Aris felt the weight of those words settle in.

"What are you suggesting?" she said, attempting to hide the shaking in her voice.

She would rather not be a pawn in someone else's game at all. But something deep inside her stirred—an increasing sense of urgency that this might be a lifeline thrown into the pandemonium.

Hassan said:

"An unlikely alliance," and her eyes narrowed

a little, as if she were thinking about how plausible that was. "You have skills and information that we require. Your knowledge of Synapse could change the game for them. But it's a risk, Aris."

As many questions raced through Aris's thoughts, the walls of the room seemed to throb with unsaid threats. Was Hassan trustworthy? What was underneath the tough appearance of this security officer? The stakes were higher than ever, and desperation made it difficult to see where trust began and ended.

"What does that mean?" she questioned, her voice stronger than she felt.

"We get inside the system," Hassan said, bending forward and speaking urgently. "We follow the manipulation. We expose them. But I need you to be ready to lose everything. Don't get me wrong; this is a risky game, and the chances are not in our favour."

For a time, Aris's mind was racing. The echoes of betrayal lingered in the air, along with the fear for her life. But the brief images of a world where her work might either make things worse or bring order back to them set something off in her.

"I'll do it," she said, her determination growing even as she could feel the weight of her future hanging by a thread.

Hassan's expression showed a hint of respect.

"Then we don't have any time to spend. The Puppeteer won't let us take a break."

With that, the chilly grip of doubt became stronger, and Aris prepared for the dangerous road ahead.

As the sun set and the streets of Dubai became dark and quiet, Aris found herself face to face with Agent Layla Hassan. Her heart raced like a faraway battle drum. Having experienced betrayal, every instinct cautioned me against trusting anyone. But here, stuck in the high-tech walls of a secure facility, she had little choice but to think about teaming up with a lady she didn't know anything about.

Hassan's gaze was piercing, taking in every detail of Aris's face as if she could peel aside the layers of her dread and loneliness. Hassan stated in a quiet but firm voice:

"You need to understand that the threads that tie this conspiracy together are dangerous. I know you believe in Synapse, but the effects of what you made go far beyond what you meant."

Aris felt the weight of Hassan's words on him like the hot, humid air around them. She had many questions in her head: How could she work with someone who lived in a world where motives were hidden behind layers of secrecy? Every word spoken felt like a raw nerve exposed, and every look reminded her of how weak she was.

As Hassan started to explain the threat they faced around the world, Aris battled to keep scepticism from growing. It wasn't just about her invention; it was a fight for the very heart of stability in a world that wanted to be chaotic. But no matter how many facts Aris heard, she couldn't shake the sense of scepticism that was eating away at her gut. Was Hassan really on her side, or had she just walked into a web of lies that was more complicated than she could have imagined?

"You've seen what the predictions have done and who they've gone after," Hassan said, her voice getting more agitated. "If we don't deal with this now, it will destroy everything we know."

Aris swallowed hard, her throat dry as she thought about the friends and coworkers that Synapse had named. Every name was a harsh reminder of what they were up against.

But even as Hassan told her the scary details, Aris couldn't stop thinking about her worries. She could no longer afford to trust.

"How do I know you're not in on this?" Aris shot back, her voice full of wrath and terror. "How can I be certain I won't be another pawn?"

There was a weighty challenge in the air between them, like an invisible wall made of the rubble of their different universes. Hassan's face softened, showing that she really understood.

"Because I've lost everything in this fight, just like you. I will do whatever to safeguard what's left, even if it means standing next to someone I don't know well."

At that time, a weak but hopeful connection sparked between them. However, months of hiding and survival had sharpened Aris's senses, warning him to exercise caution. Could she count on this union to stand up to the storms of betrayal that were waiting in the shadows? As hesitation filled her thoughts, the distant sounds of their possible enemies got closer, and Aris knew she didn't have much time left to make a choice.

Hassan said:

"We don't have time to hesitate," and there was a storm in her eyes. "We have to hit first, but I can't do it by myself."

Aris felt a shudder run down her spine as the weight of the moment sank like lead in her gut. They were on the edge of not knowing what to do, aware that any wrong move may spell disaster for them, but equally aware that working together might be their only chance to live.

As she thought about her choices, the sound

of footfall echoed down the hall, a clear sign that they were not alone. The choice was like a dark tunnel that separated what she knew from what she didn't. Aris had to make a choice: trust the shaky tie of trust or run away into the darkness, where danger was always waiting.

10
Digital Trails in the Sand

As the sun fell behind Dubai's tall towers, the shadows became longer, making a web of dark corners and hidden spaces where secrets thrived. Aris stood in the sterile light of a makeshift computer hub, her heart beating as she and Hassan began their journey into the dark web, a maze full of hazards and the unknown. The rough hum of the servers around them seemed like a storm about to break, making her mind even more unsure.

"We need to start with the data logs and figure out when the problems started," Hassan said, her fingers speeding over the computer.

The screen lit up with lines of code that Aris had never seen before. As she read the streams of information that were flowing across the screen, her stomach began to feel heavy. The problems weren't just bugs; they were well-planned threads meant to trick people.

"What if we can find the places where the injections go in?" Aris offered, her voice full of desperation. "We might find the original code if we follow them back."

But she couldn't help but feel a shiver of mistrust. What if they were already too late? Their enemy had been able to use Synapse as a weapon against her and everyone else in her area. Hassan nodded and flipped through displays, and Aris felt panic creeping up on her like a vine, trying to choke her focus.

The more they explored, the more the web's evil plan became clear. Like traps ready to catch the unwary, layers of misdirection were carefully laid.

"There! Look at this!" Hassan yelled out of nowhere, cutting through Aris's thoughts.

Aris had never seen the hidden path in the code before, but the screen showed it. It was a digital snake that wrapped around the algorithm's core.

"This could take us back to the original command input!"

Hope flashed, but a deep sense of despair gradually took over. Aris felt like somebody was watching her, and every line of code could be a way for someone to harm her.

"We need to be careful. If they find out we're spying on them..."

She didn't finish her thought, and the meaning hung in the air. Hassan's piercing stare met hers, and they both knew they had to do what they had to do. They would finish this, but the future was full of danger; they had to hurry to expose the corruption before it took over them both.

As they kept going through the huge amount of data, Hassan's terminal suddenly went off, waking them both up. Hassan said quickly:

"We've been found." Her face went from focused intent to steely resolve in an instant. "We have to go now."

Aris's heart raced, and adrenaline flooded her veins as the reality of their dangerous situation hit her hard. They had to find out the truth before it found them. It was no longer time to be careful; the chase had begun.

As the clock ticked down and the shadows grew longer around them, Aris and Hassan leaned heavily on their talents. They knew that to fight their unseen adversary, they needed more than just passion; they needed to strategically organise their resources. The elegant conference room at Hassan's Dubai office was buzzing with the quiet hum of technology. Screens were showing coded data racing over their surfaces, yet the intensity in their voices cut through the cacophony.

Hassan said:

"We have access to the most advanced surveillance tools and cyber intelligence in the region." Her voice was firm even though their lives were in chaos. "I can connect you with some of my contacts. No one knows the digital world here better than they do."

Aris nodded as she typed quickly on her laptop. Her mind was racing. The connection could mean the difference between uncovering the truth and succumbing to the conspiracy.

Aris went on to say:

" We also need to use Synapse's own algorithms. " She narrowed her eyes as she thought about what this meant. "We can use it to learn more about possible patterns of the manipulations that are aimed at us. I want to view the strands of data that have been lost in real time. If we understand who is the target and why, we can begin to plan a counterattack."

The conviction in her words softened Hassan's cold stare slightly.

Putting the parts together made the huge amount of work that lay ahead obvious. As they went deeper into the murky waters of the conspiracy, they drew the attention of invisible watchers. Aris's fingers moved quickly across the keyboard, adding code on top of code and carefully following the digital trail left by those who had messed with her work. It turned into a race against time, a high-stakes chase where failure meant death—not just for Synapse, but for everybody who tried to find out the truth.

A loud alarm went off out of nowhere, breaking their focus and lighting up the room in a bright red.

"We've been found!" Hassan yelled, showing live surveillance footage from the city.

Drones flew around the skyline like birds of prey, looking for their targets. Their camera lenses glinted in the dim light of nightfall. Aris's heart raced. They needed to take action quickly.

"Turn off anything that could give away our location. We need to go away," Hassan said, and her calmness slipped just enough to show the anxiety under her steel façade. "It's over if they find us now."

Aris immediately retraced their digital track, deleting footprints and removing all evidence of what they had done. She was full of adrenaline. But even as she followed the orders, she felt a strong sensation of dread. Who were they actually fighting? The shadows who lurked beyond the screen weren't just faceless enemies; they were the ones who made the pandemonium.

The walls felt closer, a grim reminder that every second counted in this game of survival. They had to move quickly to remain ahead of the threat that was coming. Aris's mind was racing with thoughts: technology could help them, but it could also be a weapon of evil in the wrong hands. They were in a fight much broader than either of them had thought—a war of ideas woven together in a digital tapestry that could come apart at any time, leaving destruction in its wake. Aris saw flashes of light in dark places that reminded him that in this future, trust would be as rare as daylight, and the stakes had never been higher.

Aris looked at the lines of code on the screen and fought the sensation of dread that was coming over her. Every time she pressed a key, it felt like the weight of the world was on her shoulders. The digital world opened up like a dangerous maze, with twists and turns that she didn't see coming. The more they looked into Synapse's system, the more disturbing information they found.

Aris carefully put together the pieces of falsified information with the help of Agent Hassan. She thought it was like trying to keep a house of cards from falling down, with each new piece of information threatening to ruin everything they had worked for. The algorithm that used to be a sign of optimism now turned on itself, showing its evil role in malicious plans. Hassan's critical eye analysed the patterns, and her brow furrowed as she pointed out things that Aris had missed initially.

Hassan remarked: "It's not just random targets," and her eyes narrowed in focus. "Look deeper. They are picking people out for a reason."

The implications were heavy in the air: a

bigger conspiracy made up of powerful groups that were hidden behind layers of lies. Aris had a chill run down her spine when she realised that they weren't just keeping an eye on predictions; they were also keeping an eye on individuals, controlling them, and eventually turning them into weapons.

Now, every little thing mattered. When Aris found an important node on the web of lies—an encrypted file hidden away under layers of bogus data and digital decoys—she felt a rush of adrenaline. It was a door that led to the puppeteer's plans. She muttered:

"If we can trace this info back, we might find the source.'

Hope and terror mixed in her voice. She looked Hassan in the eye, and the look on her face showed that they both needed to act quickly.

Hassan said in a serious tone:

"We have to be careful. They're watching us, and if they think we're onto them, they'll strike back."

Aris nodded, feeling that their predicament was becoming worse. The walls seemed to close in, and the machines around them suddenly became too loud. While they worked, a feeling of vulnerability spread through the room, and an undercurrent of danger indicated that something was hiding just beyond the digital barrier.

Time flew by, and every second felt like it was out of rhythm. A notice suddenly pinged on the screen, breaking the tense silence. A warning came up:

"Unauthorised access detected."

"They know we're here!" Aris shouted, her heart thumping.

She felt panic rise in her, but her trained instinct kicked in as she pushed back against the wave of fear.

Hassan said: "We need to get this data out now," and her voice was calm in the middle of the commotion.

The seconds passed like a countdown, and each one was more important than the last. Aris's fingers sped over the keyboard, perform-ing commands quickly and accurately, despite their knowledge of impending capture. The lights flickered, which was a serious indicator that their time of protection was running out.

"Hurry!" Hassan said, looking around the room quickly to check if there were any hazards he couldn't see.

Aris felt both happy and scared as the data started to move. They were close to finding out the truth, but a great force was hiding in the shadows, ready to silence them for good. The screens went dark all of a sudden, just as the last file dropped. An alarm that echoed around the room and bright red lights filled it.

"They've gotten into the system!" Hassan yelled, her heart racing with adrenaline. "Now we have to leave!"

Aris had no other choice than to go after Hassan into the mayhem, where the world around them was falling apart in terror and uncertainty. They were stuck in a web of lies, but they were determined to break free, even if it meant losing everything.

11
The Puppeteer's Game

As Aris and Hassan carefully looked over the data they had collected, the air in the small, dark room hummed with tension. Lines of code and altered algorithms flashed across the displays, and each pixel showed a dark truth that made them shiver. The truth they had uncovered was shocking. It was more than just criminal exploitation; it was a planned orchestration of mayhem by a person they had only heard rumours of: The Puppeteer.

Every time they tried to connect the dots, they got deeper into a web of lies, a dark place where shadows danced and hidden agendas thrived. It became brutally evident to Aris that the targets were not random as he figured out the patterns hidden in the algorithm. They intentionally placed players in a much bigger game. The effects were terrifying: not just people were ruined, but whole institutions were destabilised, economies were disrupted, and lives were lost.

Hassan remarked in a voice that was just above a whisper:

"It's all meant to make people scared and unsure. The Puppeteer isn't just trying to control things; they're holding the world hostage to their vision and leading us towards chaos."

Aris felt dismal reality settle in her chest as her mind raced over the interrelated layers of their data, realising how big the threat they faced was. They weren't just up against a rogue group; they were up against someone who built things to destroy.

At that moment of enlightenment, Aris felt a mix of fear and determination. The stakes had never been higher, and the road ahead needed more than just technical skill. It needed guts, determination, and a willingness to face the darkness that followed them everywhere.

"We have to expose this," she said, holding on to the edge of the table as if it could hold her down against the weight of the truth that was coming out. "We can't let The Puppeteer decide what happens to us."

Hassan nodded, and a furious determination shone in her eyes. The two were about to make a choice that may either set them free or put them in much more danger. They understood that every second they wasted made The Puppeteer stronger. They had to move quickly and use the information they had gathered to create their own counter-strategy, one that could break free from the ties of manipulation. They would work together to find the architect and stop the dark puppetry that was threatening to take over their lives.

As they got ready to carry out their plan, each person realised that the risks could take them down a path, from which they couldn't come back. But there was no denying the fire that was burning inside them—the need to take back control from an unseen enemy. They took one last look at the screens that lit up the dark room before stepping into the unknown, well aware that their lives were on the line in the game of life.

As Aris and Hassan dug deeper into the complicated web of lies that The Puppeteer had woven, the harsh truths they found began to weigh hard on her mind. What had begun as a powerful coding algorithm had turned into a sign of anarchy, which she had never meant to happen. Synapse was no longer merely a tool to stop crime; it was a ghost with weapons that haunted not just the people it anticipated but also the fundamental fabric of society.

People talked of the Puppeteer's evil plans at secret meetings held in the stifling brightness of neon lights. Synapse's predictions were meticulously planned to go after people who could upset markets, change political stories, or cause panic. Every alert that popped up on Aris's screen portrayed a story of danger and strife, portraying a dark picture of a world that was slowly heading towards disaster. It wasn't just a string of bad things that happened; it was a planned move for power. The realisation sent chills down her spine.

Aris murmured to Hassan, "This isn't just about us anymore," her voice barely above a whisper as they rushed through the glass halls of the Dubai innovation centre. "The Puppeteer is in charge of something much bigger than we thought. If we don't stop them, we'll lose Synapse, and the world will be in turmoil."

Hassan's face showed how worried she was, which showed how serious the situation was. Aris clenched her fists as the weight of her duties hit her firmly. The clock was ticking, and with each passing second, their enemy's hold grew stronger, trapping the Earth in darkness.

As they looked at the data, patterns developed like a scary symphony, with notes of fear, greed, and manipulation playing together to create a dissonant reality. Aris felt a sense of regret, gnawing at her determination as she learnt more. She thought about how many innocent people would be hurt when the Puppeteer's perfectly planned facade fell apart. As they peeled back each layer, the stakes got higher, and the distinctions between friend and enemy became even more blurry.

"We need to let people know about this," Aris said, her heart beating with desperation. "We need to let the world know what's really going on."

But amid the twisted shadows of power and lies, they were darker and longer than she had thought they would be. They had no idea that trouble was on the way, and as they got closer to the heart of the Puppeteer's business, an even bigger threat loomed—one that may destroy them all.

After a lot of hard work, Aris and Hassan's findings concerning The Puppeteer have become obvious. The data that used to look like a harmless computational tool for safety had changed into something much worse: a weaponised matrix of chaos that was causing social unrest. The effects of this distortion made the air surrounding them tense enough to cut through the thick silence of the Dubai night.

The Puppeteer meticulously planned his strategy, viewing chaos as a form of art he could integrate into the fabric of civilisation. By choosing targets in the upper echelons of power and respectability, Aris realised that the puppeteer wasn't just trying to increase violence; he wanted to destabilise whole markets, cause political crises, and create a global environment of terror. As Aris peered at the glowing screen, the pattern of forecasts began to look like a creepy dance, with each prediction playing its part in a bigger show put on by the Puppeteer.

It was evident, more than ever, how urgent their situation was. The Puppeteer was strengthening his grip because he knew that Aris and Hassan were getting closer to the reality he wanted to hide so badly. They had to do something before the darkness reached them again and pandemonium turned into destruction. With a flick of her wrist, Hassan started to explain their strategy to go to the heart of the plot—the nerve centre that drove Synapse. As their hearts raced and their adrenaline rose, they both raced against an unseen clock, knowing that the next step could either take them deeper into darkness or set them free.

As they got ready for the last time, Aris felt the weight of what was to come on his shoulders. She was no longer merely a programmer whose job it was to make predictive technology; she was a key player in a far bigger fight for power over the future itself. And every step in the dark tango between freedom and manipulation was important.

A scary thought broke through her determination. What happens when things get out of control? What if the puppeteer won?

12

Closing in on the Threat

Dark clouds hung over Dubai, which was a sign of the rising tension on the ground. As Aris's resolve grew stronger, she could feel the Puppeteer's shadow getting heavier. Every step she took across the busy city brought her closer to the edge of danger. There was a torrent of threats whispering through the crowded streets, and the flashing neon lights and never-ending sirens made it much worse. Every face she passed seemed to be watching her, and every bend seemed like a trap.

The darkly lit café made her heart race as she talked to Hassan through a secure channel. Their plan of action became both her lifeline and her worst peril.

Hassan said:

"They know we're onto something," her voice steady but with a sense of urgency. "If the Puppeteer knows, it won't be easy to get in."

Aris thought about what it meant, remembering the scary things that had happened in the preceding few weeks. They faced more than just an anonymous algorithm; a careful architect of chaos had ensnared them in a web. Hassan told them what to do next to strengthen their new alliance and defences, but Aris couldn't shake the impression that the adversary was already one step ahead.

The peace inside the café was broken when people outside started yelling. Aris leapt to her feet, her heart pounding, as shadows swiftly passed by the windows. She cried:

"We've been compromised!" as adrenaline pumped through her body.

They had to go before they became targets. Hassan and Aris looked at each other with determination and ran to the back exit. A tight knot of excitement held them back as they were ready to navigate the city's maze-like back lanes. They knew that revenge from the shadows was going to happen, but they were determined to face their foes head-on, ready for whatever that might be.

As they walked through the small alleyways, the night closing in on them, every choice felt important. Aris groped for the encrypted gadget in her pocket. Her mind was spinning with numbers and possible plans, like fireflies that only show up in a dark place. The stakes were too enormous to bear. They weren't only trying to stay alive; they were fighting for the future of Synapse and the truth itself. Every heartbeat echoed the truth that the time for revenge was now, as the net surrounding them got tighter.

Aris peered over the table in their Dubai safe

house, which was poorly lit and covered in digital maps and hurriedly written notes. Her mind was racing. She felt like the walls were closing in on her as she thought about the pandemonium going on outside. Just a few days ago, they were at the forefront of an amazing piece of technology. Now, it was a weapon that was being used against them, and with each tick of the clock, the stakes got higher.

Hassan said with unwavering determination:

"We need to change how we do things." Her gaze looked over Aris's face, looking for any sign of hesitation. "We can't keep waiting for the Puppeteer to make the next move. We need to hit them first."

Aris nodded, and the tension in her chest grew. The feeling of fear that she was used to came back, but she pushed it down. There wasn't enough time to think about it. Aris felt a chill run down her spine as they planned their next move. Each link they made on the digital flowchart showed how important the situation was to them personally. It was no longer just about finding the heart of Synapse that might be used to control people; it was about staying alive. A mistake could cost her everything: her life, her work, and the people she had come to trust. She put the scary thoughts out of her mind and concentrated on the little things.

Aris said:

"If we can get to the main server before they know what we're doing, we'll have the upper hand." Her voice became stronger as she spoke. "We'll put a stop to their tricks with a countermeasure."

Hassan nodded, her face hard, and they started to plan how to get in. Plans moved from one level of approval to another, from computerised designs to possible threats, and every word was full of urgency. Aris looked at the screen that showed the complicated network of links. The more she looked into the black threads of data, the more evil the puppeteering seemed. Could they find their way through this maze without becoming stuck? Their determination grew stronger as the night went on. Now they were warriors, fighting an enemy they couldn't see who was eager to use terror as a weapon to seize control.

The mood changed all of a sudden. An electronic alert went off in the room, and both women stopped what they were doing. Hassan quickly went to look into it, and they gave each other tense stares. She affirmed in a voice just above a whisper:

"It's coming from their last known location."

Aris felt a rush of adrenaline as they realised how serious the situation was. They couldn't wait any longer; every second mattered. Aris's fingers shook as she tightened her grasp on the mouse.

"We're going to recalibrate right here and now. We need to catch them before they catch us. "

With quick clicks, she started changing the algorithms in Synapse so that it might use its predictive powers to find the Puppeteer's next target. The tension was thick; every heartbeat in the quiet room seemed to echo with a sense of impending conflict. Aris thought about it while the screen flickered, lighting up their determined features. Would their new mission work? Or will they get even more stuck in the Puppeteer's twisted game? With their determination growing, they got ready for the unknown ahead. They felt like the world was on their shoulders and knew that their next move may change the balance of power forever.

Aris stood at the window of the little hotel room in Dubai and looked out at the neon lights below, which made her face glow. There was a storm developing in the digital world, and they were right in the middle of it. The charts she had gotten from Synapse's backend danced on her laptop screen. Each line told a story of turmoil, and each spike was a heartbeat in the conspiracy they were trying to figure out. Hassan walked in with a blank look on her face, but Aris could tell that she was tense.

"We have to go. The Puppeteer knows we know what he's up to. The security measures he's put in place are already getting tighter around us. We can't stay here for long."

Aris barely heard the warning since her mind was racing with what the facts on her screen meant. If we can figure out who the next targets are, we might have enough to catch him. What if this is the only chance we have? She pointed to the most recent analysis.

" Check this out: these algorithms didn't just guess what would happen. They were made to make a crisis worse. It's planned panic, and it goes straight to London."

Hassan went closer, and her eyes carefully looked over the information Aris had given her.

"London. We need to go back there and meet up with Corbin again. He needs to know what we've discovered. The Puppeteer's actions affect the whole world, not just a small area. Before he strikes again, we need to set up a clear way to talk to each other."

"Then we leave now," Aris said, her heart racing with adrenaline. Any second they spent looking at the data was another second wasted, and the Puppeteer could counter any action they made. "We can't let him mess up the city too much."

As Hassan got ready for their escape, Aris's fingers raced quickly over the keyboard, sending the important charts to a safe drive. But as soon as she hit save, a warning sprang up on the screen. A warning from Synapse that made her stomach turn with fear. Someone was looking at their data and following their digital trails.

"Hassan!" Aris gasped, and you could hear how urgent her voice was. " We have to go. Now."

The two women rushed towards the door, but as they stepped outside, they saw two dark figures emerging from the lift, their intentions clear. The Puppeteer's net had once again ensnared them, and this time, escape seemed impossible.

Hassan instinctively drew her weapon, but Aris grabbed her arm.

"We can't fight them here. We need a better way to escape. We have time to get to the service staircase before they spot us."

At that moment of panic, she remembered the fire escape at the end of the corridor, which could serve as their lifeline.

They turned on their heels and ran down the corridor towards the back staircase. Aris's heart raced as they went down. Every flight seemed to last forever as footsteps boomed behind them, pushing them to keep going. Her goal felt heavy on her shoulders, and the adrenaline made it hard for her to see clearly. She knew that failing would have serious ramifications.

They stepped out into the alley behind the hotel and were hit by the crisp night air, which seemed full of urgency. There were huge buildings of technology all around them, but now they were in a dire situation.

"We'll have to go a different way to get to the airport."

Hassan scanned the darkness for any indications of danger and declared,

"We will closely monitor the main roads."

A siren suddenly broke the silence of the night, echoing off the smooth walls. Aris stopped in her tracks, her gut sense taking over, and ran deeper into Dubai's maze-like alleys.

There were shouts in the distance, and the chase started again. This time, it was much more than just staying alive; it was about finding out the truth that had trapped them all.

13
Threads of Unity

Aris crossed the bridge into London with her heart beating as the fog rolled over the Thames. The voyage she had to take was quite hard on her shoulders. It was no longer merely a fight to get her technology back; it was about staying alive. She thought about Hassan, the tough security guard from Dubai. Would she trust her in this shaky partnership? Time would tell.

Detective Inspector Miles Corbin, on the other hand, was at his desk in the precinct, and the blinking notifications from Synapse were cutting through his day like a knife. The predictive algorithm he had been so doubtful about suddenly looked like the key to getting to the bottom of the web of lies that was jeopardising his cases and maybe even his life.

He had to look at the patterns again to see if they could get him closer to the centre of the scheme, as he trusted Synapse. Everyone in the room turned to look at Aris when the door opened. The tension was thick.

Corbin said:

"You could have kept running, but you came here." His voice was full of doubt, but it was also full of determination. "Your guesses are already making things harder for us to figure out. The potential for confusion is huge."

Aris nodded, knowing that meeting in person

was a dangerous thing to do. But when she told Corbin about the convoluted threads of manipulation that had brought her here, she saw a flash of hope in his steely eyes.

Hassan walked in, her demeanour calm and calculating. The tension in the room grew as she looked Aris and Corbin in the eye.

"We need to combine our data. The Puppeteer is not just any enemy; he knows how to manage data. Therefore, we have to keep one step ahead of him."

The uneasy alliances started to form as they talked about their ideas. Sofia Petrova's warning rang in Aris's head: without a moral foundation, their joint project could go wrong like Synapse did. There was a profound quiet in the room. What rules would help them make their choices? Every minute they spent not knowing what would happen made the net around them tighter.

Then, Aris looked out the window at the street, and her instincts kicked in. Time was running out. We can't wait much longer. She urged us to act quickly if we wanted to stop the Puppeteer, even though she could feel uncertainty creeping into her voice.

Corbin took a big breath.

"We're all in this together, but we need a plan. Something real before it's too late. The clock is ticking, and the danger is real," he said, his conviction cutting through the strain.

The room was filled with shaky determination.

"Let's use your knowledge of the area and my tech skills," Aris said, her voice clear now that she was full of adrenaline.

They were eager to work together, since the stakes had never been higher. But the Puppeteer was already planning their downfall from the shadows. As the city lights began to glitter against the darkening sky, a sense of anarchy loomed just out of grasp.

In the middle of London, a secret meeting took place in a dark conference room. The air was thick with suspense and excitement. Aris, Corbin, and Hassan sat around a shiny table, their faces showing how heavy the choices they had to make were. Sofia Petrova stood in front of them, her presence grounding as she looked at the high-tech instruments and data reports that showed what they had found. Every piece of evidence they found pointed to a terrifying truth: an unknown hand was controlling Synapse and using its predictions for a much worse purpose.

Sofia started:

"This isn't just a technological mistake." Her voice was steady but full of urgency. "The effects of what we've seen are huge. If someone uses Synapse for their own or political benefit, the disruption it may cause would be much worse than any crime prediction model. We're on the edge of a moral cliff."

The seriousness of her comments hovered in the air, sparking a heated debate among the group.

Corbin crossed his arms, showing how law enforcement usually thinks.

"But isn't the chance to stop crime worth the risk? Isn't that the point of all this?" he asked, his brow furrowing as he tried to make sense of his instinct to protect the public and the growing evidence that morality was being compromised.

"You're speaking in absolutes, Miles," Aris said, his voice solid with conviction. "The technology itself isn't bad; it's how people choose to use it that is. We know how easy it is to change data. Take a look at the profiles Synapse detected. Each one is like a pawn on a chessboard that we are only starting to figure out."

As the talks got out of hand, the air became tense. Hassan, always the realist, leaned in and looked at her allies with a stern glance.

"What is our moral high ground if we don't watch out? Every choice we make could ruin the lives of innocent people, or worse. We need to question ourselves, are we becoming what we hate by fighting this puppeteer?"

Her inquiry was so serious that it made them all think about what their objective really was.

With each exchange, the group's excitement faded as the moral grey areas grew. It was clear that there was a tension, and each ally was struggling with what their partnership would bring. In a society dominated by data, could they trust themselves not to become the very thing they were trying to destroy?

At that point, it was evident that the struggle they were getting ready for wasn't just against an unseen enemy; it was also against the morals that guided all of their choices.

"We need to come to an agreement," Sofia said, her voice calm in the middle of the maelstrom. "If we don't make this mission clear in terms of ethics, we could let something much worse than we can imagine happen. I need each of you to say what you're willing to give up for the greater good."

As her words rang in the room, they felt the heavy weight of responsibility on their shoulders. They had to face not only the outside enemy, but also the internal fight that may get in the way of their quest for justice.

The argument was like a storm of ideas and fears, and the stakes got higher with each passing instant. They didn't know it, but time wasn't on their side. The Puppeteer stayed in the shadows, knowing that their plans were falling apart. As time went on, the need for clarity and unity became more and more urgent. They were running out of time to either find their moral compass or deal with the terrible things that would happen if they didn't.

The air was thick with unresolved questions, and Sofia stood in the dark light of the conference room, her form silhouetted against the sleek glass windows of the London skyline. Years of experience encircled her like a cloud. Aris, Corbin, and Hassan all felt a change in the air as she began to talk. Her voice was calm but full of urgency.

Sofia started by saying:

"We often don't think about how our new ideas will affect things." Her blue eyes cut through the cloud of doubt. "The same algorithms that can predict criminal behaviour can also be used as weapons by people who want to gain power. Aris, you've created a useful tool, but keep in mind that it can serve multiple purposes."

Corbin leaned in and furrowed his brow.

"We need to know what we're up against. We must not underestimate the potential misuse of Synapse, especially if the Puppeteer is as intelligent as you suggest."

"Exactly," Sofia said, looking back and forth between the three of them. "The similarities in history are scary. People with malicious intentions have always been interested in powerful technologies. Always. Think about what will happen when predictive policing turns into predictive persecution."

Aris felt a cold shiver travel down her spine. The stress of her past experiences came rushing back, making her think about the innocent lives that would be damaged by what she had made.

"But it's supposed to help people," she said, her voice full of desperation. "The goal was to protect, predict, and stop crime!"

Sofia's face relaxed a little, but the need was still there.

"Yes, but think about what 'crime' means and who gets to decide what it means. Prepare yourself for the possibility that someone is already using your algorithm to incorrectly target individuals."

Hassan, who was paying attention to the conversation, said:

"If we're going to expose this conspiracy, we need to use Sofia's ideas to come up with a plan. Before we can stop Synapse, we need to know how it is being used."

"Right," Aris said, her determination rising to the surface. "Let's change how we do things.

I need to look more closely at the data we've gathered. There might be something we've missed."

At that moment, the mood changed suddenly, nearly without anyone noticing. There was an electric tension in the air as each of them took in how serious their situation was. The rain in London fell steadily outside, making the commotion outdoors match the mayhem within.

Sofia moved closer, and the intensity of her face showed.

"Aris, keep your purpose in mind: how you use your technology can either help or hurt communities. Your adventure is more than just a fight against the Puppeteer; it's also about finding out what your creation's moral duty is. Your actions don't just affect you; they affect the story that shapes our future."

As she spoke, Aris felt a sudden bolt of understanding. It was no longer just about stopping a conspiracy; it was a strong call to action. They were on the verge of something huge, but the damage they were about to do might be worse than the solutions they were looking for.

As they all understood the factors working against them, the room felt smaller. The clock was ticking down. The Puppeteer did not back down, and at that point, the stakes became very evident. They all stood at the brink, holding on to the thin thread that kept them together, knowing that the next step may either start their fight or end it for good.

14
Confrontation at the Core

Aris moved her earphone around and looked around the dimly lit control room, her heart racing. The air was tense, and every beat echoed the quick thrum of her heart. She could see the determination on the faces of Hassan and Corbin as they prepared the technical equipment. They had limited time and a risky plan to enter the centre of Synapse. Every second mattered.

The three of them had spent hours going over security protocols and surveillance feeds. To get to the heart of the operation, they had to take advantage of every weakness.

Hassan remarked:

"We need to move quickly." Her voice was calm even though the time was quite tense. "We'll only have a few minutes to turn off the algorithm before the alarm goes off once we're inside."

Aris nodded and bit her lip, feeling the weight of her creation on her. Synapse, which was supposed to protect, had become a weapon against the people it was supposed to save. She said:

"If we can get to the main server, I can rewrite the algorithm and stop the manipulation." Each syllable was full of urgency. "We just need to work together and look out for each other."

They all grasped their roles with only one look. Corbin and Hassan would take care of security by diverting the guards, while Aris used her coding skills to get through the maze-like systems that once seemed so familiar but were now strange and twisted. Aris felt a tremble of anxiety and worry as she went for the keyboard. But now was not the time to doubt. They were now too near to turn back.

At first, the air was full with hope, but as they got closer to the secure room, the mood changed. Aris could hear her heart beating faster, each beat reminding her of how important it was. The hallway ahead was dark and scary, with shadows moving in and out of the bright lights above. An unexpected sound, like metal clanging, bounced off the walls and made her catch her breath. It was a brief reminder that danger was always there, just out of sight.

"Be careful," Corbin said quietly, looking around the hallway with his sharp eyes. "We can't make any mistakes."

The words hung in the air, making the strain that was already building in Aris's chest much worse. They continued onwards, each step a fight against the fear that was pounding in their heads and threatening to break through their calm.

When they got to the door of the core chamber, Aris could practically feel the technology behind it beating. She felt a strong connection inside her, bittersweet like an echo of what could have been. With shaking hands, she opened the security panel, her fingers moving quickly over the keys as she broke through layers of encryption. The rush of adrenaline was acute and focused.

The door suddenly hissed open, and the three of them walked in. For a second, Aris couldn't breathe—her creation's lifeblood pumped around her in the whir of machines and the cool brightness of displays. This was her space, yet it felt strange, very different from what she had imagined. The weight of their quest sank in her stomach like an anchor.

"I'm in," she shouted, her voice full of urgency as she typed into the server interface. "I'll change the main algorithm, but I need some time..."

The words faded away as a red light began to flash above them, and a siren rang through the room, breaking the fragile moment of control.

"We have to go! Now!" Hassan yelled, immediately telling Corbin to cover their escape.

Aris's eyes moved quickly from the code on the screen to the door. Every second felt heavier than the last. She couldn't stand the thought of failing; too many people depended on the decisions they made in the next few minutes.

The countdown of danger pushed Aris to her limits as she typed feverishly. The Puppeteer was out there, and they were right in the middle of everything he had made. Even though alarms were going off and security forces were rushing towards them, the thought made her more determined.

"Stay in the queue!" Corbin yelled as he got ready to fight the menace that was coming.

Aris looked at him quickly, feeling both thankful and scared. She had the chance to change the algorithm's fate right then and there. They were on the edge, and the outcome was up in the air. All she could think about were the lives that were still hidden in the shadows of her work.

It was clear that there was a lot of tension in the air as Aris, Corbin, and Hassan stood in front of the Synapse Solutions central data hub. Their hearts raced in time with the clock above them, and every second was full of the possible implications of failure. Aris had always believed in Synapse's promise, which was a light of hope in predictive technology, but now it felt like a ghost—a wicked spirit that wanted to eat them all.

They had carefully planned their way in, moving through layers of security and digital traps that had been set up to catch them. As time went on, the stakes got higher. The Puppeteer had turned her invention into a weapon, and the data that might control millions of lives was getting harder and harder to get. The complicated dance of technology was no longer just a theory; it was happening right now, and they were the only ones who could stop it.

When they walked into the clean, modern halls of the data centre, the hum of servers filled the air, a dissonant symphony of power feeding the very algorithm that had deceived her. Aris said:

"We need to get to the mainframe."

Her voice was firm even though she was full of adrenaline. Corbin nodded and looked around for any sign of resistance. Hassan was just as alert and had her weapon drawn, preparing for the fight that everyone knew was coming.

As Aris linked her device to the nearest terminal, she said, "Here we go."

Her fingers flew over the keys as she tried to break through the digital defences that had been set up to keep individuals like her out. She felt the weight of the moment: years of work, noble intentions that had gone wrong, everything left bare for everyone to see. As she started a diagnostic run, she felt a mix of confusion and resolve, pushing away the anxieties that had been nagging at her.

Suddenly, alarms went off all across the building, breaking the tension like a knife. The red lights flashing made their already hectic goal even more urgent.

"We've been hacked!" Corbin yelled and instinctively took a defensive stance.

The door they had just come through slammed shut, trapping them inside and making them realise how dangerous their situation was. Every second counted, and the Puppeteer's gents would be right after them.

"Focus!" Hassan yelled, cutting through the noise. "We can't let them mess up the process."

Aris's heart raced in sync with her frantic thoughts. Her fingers flew over the touchpad, and lines of code fell in front of her like a waterfall of jumbled information. Each piece was a piece of the puzzle; she needed to put things back in order.

While she worked, a strange feeling settled in her stomach. The coding patterns made her feel uneasy because they were familiar, like an echo from the past. She had trouble breathing as memories of Ethan came flooding back. She shook her head and said, "Could it be?" Not now, not here. But as the test results came in, she realised, with a terrible feeling, that hidden backdoors had been built into Synapse's architecture by someone who had been close to her the whole time.

There were many footsteps behind them, and the growl of voices got louder. Time was up.

"Aris, can you break into the core?" Corbin yelled over the noise, and his voice showed how urgent he was. "We need to turn it off before they get here!"

"I'll try," she said, her voice firm but shaking with terror.

Her heart raced as the digital world sprang to life in front of her. She could sense the Puppeteer's evil presence inside Synapse's architecture, like a wicked puppeteer pulling strings from the darkness. It was time to take back what she had made, change its fate, and, if necessary, destroy what had taken so much from her.

As she typed, she moved deeper into the system, and the sounds of mayhem echoed along the hallway. She was no longer just battling for herself; she was fighting for honesty, for the lives at stake, and maybe most importantly, for a future where technology could be used for good instead of as a tool of manipulation. The last battle had begun, and she was the one who would decide who won.

The bright fluorescent lights in the middle of London's data centre flickered in a scary way, creating shadows that moved across the smooth walls. Aris, Corbin, and Hassan crouched behind a row of humming servers, their breaths coming in time with each other in a subtle but urgent way. Aris could hear each heartbeat in her ears as she whispered important last-minute changes to the plan. They had gone deep into enemy territory, yet the issue of who The Puppeteer was still hung heavily in the air.

The tension was thick in the air. Every second brought The Puppeteer closer to realising they were under attack. Corbin's eyes moved quickly across the dark room, which was full of operatives from an unknown enemy. Their presence was an unspoken menace hanging over them. Hassan maintained a finger on her ear, listening carefully for any news from the outside. She looked calm, but inside she was a storm.

15
Aftermath and Awakening

As the dust began to settle, Aris felt the weight of what had happened. There was a heavy silence in the air that made me feel both trapped and free. She stood in the middle of the mess, her breath shallow as she looked at the stark results of the fight. The code of Synapse, which used to be smooth and flexible, was now a broken mirror of its original function, lying at her feet like a broken glass sculpture. The world outside was dealing with the news—the media frenzy, the calls for responsibility, and the heated ethical discussions between engineers and lawmakers. And she was in the epicentre, a hesitant figure amid the storm of scrutiny.

Despite the immediate danger having gone, the conflict had left scars that ran far deeper than the physical wounds on her body. Aris knew deep down that the worst loss was not just the technology she had made, but also the trust she had broken. She thought about Ethan, who had once been her friend but was now a ghost of treachery following her around. Was her drive so strong that she didn't see what would happen? The excitement of new ideas had faded, leaving behind a scary question: When does technology turn into a weapon? The critics' voices grew louder and louder in her head as time went on. The moral issues sur-

rounding predictive policing and data manipulation were no longer simply ideas; they were
already a part of her life.

Shadows outside her window became long
and deep, as if the whole city were mourning
the loss of innocence. Aris felt a heaviness in
her chest, a recognition of how her work had
touched other people's lives. She couldn't stop
thinking about the faces that had shown up in
the bad forecasts, people who had been caught
up in a web of manipulation without knowing it.
They were more than numbers; they were real
individuals. As she thought about it, she saw
that real control came at a high cost—not just
the moral consequences, but also the emotion-
al toll it took on those who had it.

Aris was determined to take back her story
and said she wouldn't let her mistakes define
her. She understood she had to speak up for
ethical technology and guide the discourse towards responsibility and accountability in innovation. She felt a new determination building
inside her as she got ready to face the torrent of
questions that was coming. She had saved the
world from destruction, but the battle for moral
integrity in technology was just beginning. Aris
got ready; she wouldn't let the cost of control
get in the way of the chance for positive change.

Aris sat in a darkly lit chamber as the bustle around her began to calm down. The weight of her voyage was heavy on her shoulders. The fight with The Puppeteer left a jagged scar on her once-hopeful view of technology. The world outside was still full of life, but for Aris, time seemed to stand still, stuck in the echoes of treachery and the price of power.

The news had broken much more than Synapse; it had ripped away the shield of ignorance that had kept her goals safe. She looked at the screens in front of her, which were full of news about investigations into the plot, power struggles in the boardrooms, and scared individuals who were about to lose their freedom. She had unknowingly become a vital part of a game that was far bigger than she had planned.

However, in the middle of the mess, a spark of determination lit up inside her. It was the strong voice buried deep under layers of self-doubt that called for change, for a way to connect her new grasp of technology with moral responsibility. Aris saw a future where algorithms weren't used as weapons in the dark, but as instruments to give people power and keep them safe instead of taking advantage of them.

She grabbed her notepad and started writing down the ideas that were racing through her head like a storm. Plans for making technology more ethical, rules for being open, and programmes to teach both producers and consumers about the effects of their digital footprints. The conflict hadn't concluded yet; it had transitioned into a new stage, requiring individuals to advocate for responsible innovation.

As Aris wrote plans for a foundation that would focus on developing ethical AI, she could feel the adrenaline running through her veins. She used her platform to raise awareness and argue for rules that put human rights ahead of corporate margins. She knew that her determination had to go beyond her past mistakes; the mission was about making a future where freedom didn't have to be sacrificed for security.

She understood that the trip ahead would not be simple since there would be people who thrived on manipulation who would try to stop her. But with each word she wrote, she strengthened not only her goals, but also the friendships she had made during hard times. The memories of treachery that still haunted her reminded her to stay alert, but her desire to move forward pushed her on.

Aris felt clear-headed as she strengthened her grip on the pen, eager to make her vision a reality in the ever-changing world of technology. The darkness couldn't stop her; it would merely be a blank slate for the new route she was going to make. At that moment of strong reflection, she finally saw how much her decisions would affect others. This understanding gave her the will to make sure they would lead to a better dawn for everyone.

The ashes of war hung heavily in the air, covering London like a thick fog that wouldn't go away. Aris stood on the edge of a cliff and looked down at the huge city below. The sun illuminated its skyline, casting a melancholic glow over the ruins of a civilisation on the verge of anarchy. Her heart felt heavy with the weight of her choices, and every beat echoed the echoes of mistakes she had made in the past and the consequences that were about to happen. She had gone deep into the darkest corners of technology, where she had unlimited power that could do a lot of good or a lot of evil.

Corbin stood next to her, looking through the debris of their conflict with a mix of fear and determination on his weathered face.

"We fought to get back in charge, but the question is, at what cost?" he said, his voice full of doubts he didn't say out loud.

They all had wounds from the fight, some of which were easy to see and some of which were hidden. The price of their chase wrapped around them like a snake, waiting to strike. As they looked at what had happened, it was evident that their voyage had shown them much more than only the hazards of becoming complacent in invention. It had also shown them the heavy obligations that come with being a creator.

Aris turned to Sofia, the moral compass she had been looking for during their long and difficult struggle, in a last-ditch effort to fight ignorance.

"How do we make sure that the systems we make never turn into weapons against the people they were meant to protect?"

Her breathing sped up. The last fight had shaken her to her core, and she couldn't stop contemplating the shift in her fate. Sofia's voice had always sounded wise, and now it felt like an anchor in the storm.

"We need to push for openness, Aris. We need to do more than just make technology; we also need to build systems that make it possible for people to be held accountable."

A spark of determination lit up inside her as she thought about what Sofia had said.

"Then that's what I'll do," Aris said, her voice shaky but strong, and she felt a new feeling of purpose growing inside her.

She thought about how Synapse had changed people's lives and how families had been ripped apart by threats that were getting closer and closer because of her work. She couldn't hide in the exciting possibilities of innovation anymore; the risks were too high. She thought that responsibility wasn't just something you had to do; it was a guiding concept and a call to action for a future that needed to be protected.

Aris's mind raced as they got ready to face a society that was empty because of dread. She didn't know what would happen next, but she sensed a deep change inside herself. She felt a renewed sense of hope in the face of despair and a dedication to making sure that progress was ethical instead of technological tyranny. The full weight of possible threats was looming just beyond their immediate horizon, but together they would work to shine a light on the dark corners of invention, making sure that they and others were held accountable. Their adventure was far from complete, and the battle to get back control had only just begun.